Angelique: Book Four

ANGEL IN THE SNOW

CORA TAYLOR

PENGUIN CANADA

Published by the Penguin Group

Penguin Group (Canada), 90 Eglinton Avenue East, Suite 700, Toronto, Ontario, Canada M4P 2Y3
(a division of Pearson Canada Inc.)

Penguin Group (USA) Inc., 375 Hudson Street, New York, New York 10014, U.S.A.
Penguin Books Ltd, 80 Strand, London WC2R 0RL, England
Penguin Ireland, 25 St Stephen's Green, Dublin 2, Ireland (a division of Penguin Books Ltd)
Penguin Group (Australia), 250 Camberwell Road, Camberwell, Victoria 3124, Australia
(a division of Pearson Australia Group Pty Ltd)
Penguin Books India Pvt Ltd, 11 Community Centre, Panchsheel Park, New Delhi – 110 017, India
Penguin Group (NZ), cnr Airborne and Rosedale Roads, Albany, Auckland 1310, New Zealand
(a division of Pearson New Zealand Ltd)
Penguin Books (South Africa) (Pty) Ltd, 24 Sturdee Avenue, Rosebank, Johannesburg 2196,
South Africa

Penguin Books Ltd, Registered Offices: 80 Strand, London WC2R 0RL, England

First published 2006

1 2 3 4 5 6 7 8 9 10 (WEB)

Manufactured in Canada.

LIBRARY AND ARCHIVES CANADA CATALOGUING IN PUBLICATION

Taylor, Cora, 1936–
Angel in the snow / Cora Taylor.

(Our Canadian girl)
"Angelique: book four".
ISBN-13: 978-0-14-305480-1
ISBN-10: 0-14-305480-5

1. Métis—Juvenile fiction. I. Title. II. Series.

PS8589.A883A833 2006 jC813'.54 C2006-900904-X

Visit the Penguin Group (Canada) website at **www.penguin.ca**

Special and corporate bulk purchase rates available; please see
www.penguin.ca/corporatesales or call 1-800-399-6858, ext. 477 or 474

To

Mark Calette, Rose-Marie Carey,
and the other wonderful staff members
at Batoche National Historic Site

My granddaughters, Adrienne Livingston
and Emily Thomas

And my great-granddaughter, Rachel Vida

Yukon
Northwest Territories
Nunavut
British Columbia
Alberta
Saskatchewan
Manitoba

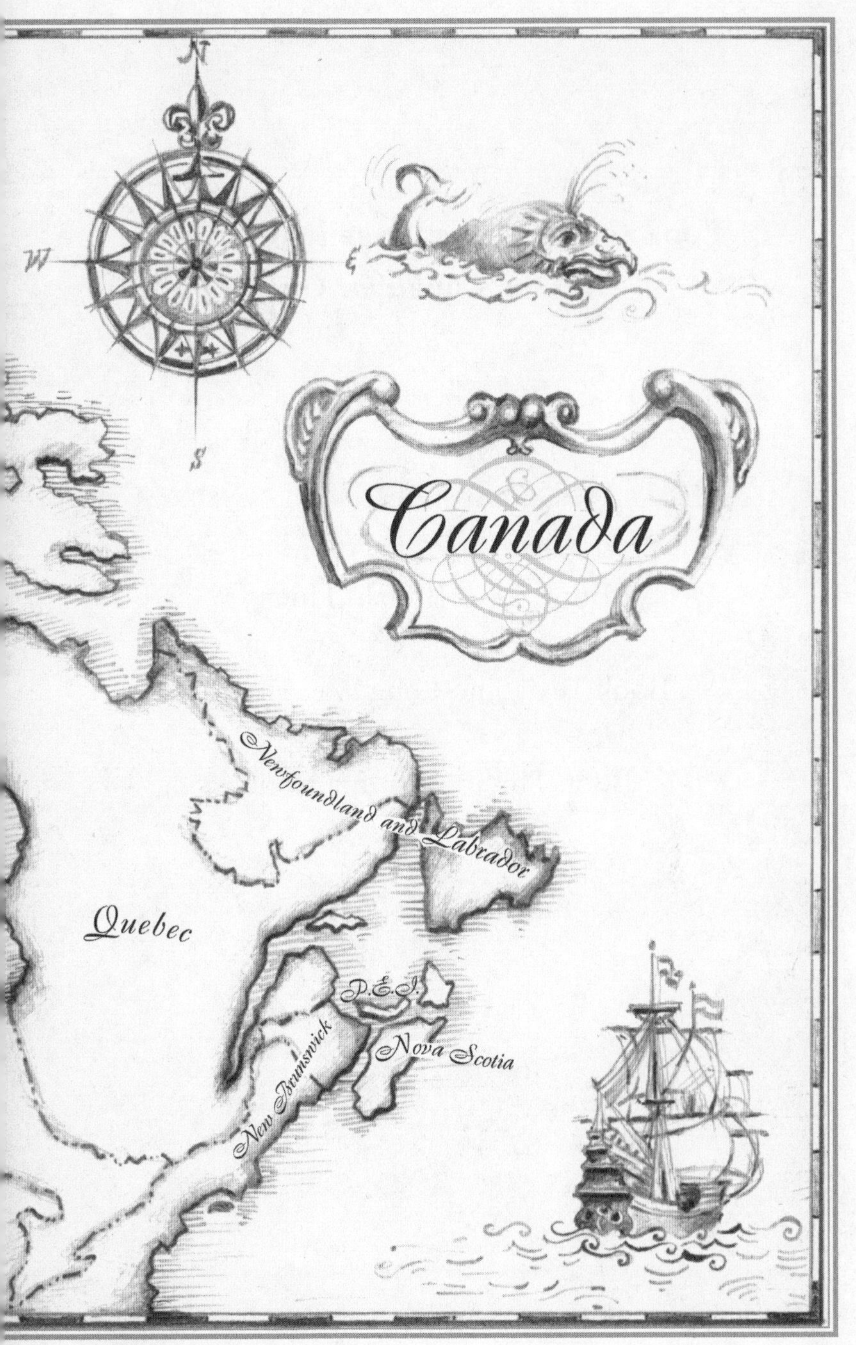

 Marks the location of the story

Look for the other Angelique stories in Our Canadian Girl

Book One: Buffalo Hunt

Book Two: The Long Way Home

Book Three: Autumn Alone

Angelique's Story Concludes

We have followed Angelique Dumas through one year of her life. In the spring, when she and her family took part in a buffalo hunt, she was almost killed while saving her brother from a wounded buffalo. She was fine, but her father's buffalo runner, Michif, was gored. Angelique dedicated herself to nursing the horse back to health.

In the summer, Michif was stolen by horse raiders and Angelique's attempt to rescue him resulted in her being kidnapped by the raiders. Her only way to escape was by riding Michif—a daring plan and the most thrilling moment of Angelique's life.

The fall hunt was a sad time for Angelique. She was left behind to care for her mother, who was having a difficult pregnancy. Angelique triumphed by riding a wild horse to get help when her mother needed it, but the men returned from the hunt with terrible news: her cousin's husband had been killed and so had her beloved Michif.

Winter can be harsh on the prairies. In this final story, Angelique learns there is more than one kind of angel in the snow.

Although the story of the fictional Angelique ends with this book, the story of the Metis settlement of Batoche continues.

In 1885, under the leadership of Louis Riel, the protest against the redivision of Metis lands culminated in tragedy for the residents of Batoche. Petitions to Ottawa were generally ignored or received vague responses. The major response was to send a force of some eight hundred fifty men under General Middleton. In addition to this force, the makers of the Gatling gun sent a gun and a man to operate it. It was the first time this early form of machine gun would be tested on human beings!

Against this formidable force, Gabriel Dumont had fewer than three hundred men (ranging in age from their early teens to their seventies) armed with hunting rifles and muskets. Dumont lost the argument with Riel concerning the means of confrontation. Gabriel wanted to draw on his men's knowledge of the land and use guerrilla warfare, attacking the army as it camped or marched. Riel vetoed this, insisting instead that they fortify the town of Batoche and fight army to army.

The result, of course, was predictable. The Metis—hopelessly outnumbered and out of ammunition (they were forced in the end to load their muskets with rocks and bits of nails)—were defeated.

Today you can visit the original townsite of Batoche and see the church and the remains of the rifle pits near Mission Hill. You can follow the trail to the site of the original ferry, the road where Angelique and Joseph raced in Book Three, or read the familiar names on the tombstones on Cemetery Hill. Some of the young guides at the wonderful Interpretive Centre are descendants of the original settlers of Batoche.

CHAPTER No 1

"It sounds as if there is some fierce animal outside. Don't you think so, Angelique?" Joseph rubbed his finger against the frosted windowpane, trying to clear a spot to peer through as the wind howled and whined around their cabin.

Winter had come with a vengeance to the little settlement at Batoche. Angelique could imagine icy claws trying to pry away the clay Papa had used to chink between the logs of their cabin. And when the clay was gone, the creature would slither through and freeze their very bones. Still, she wasn't about to let her little brother know it worried her.

"François's *kokum* says there is a *Wendigo* that walks on nights like this." She narrowed her eyes and made her voice as spooky as she could. "It is probably not an animal at all but a *Wendigo* come to get *you*!"

"Angelique!" Her cousin Thérèse had been sitting so quietly in the late afternoon darkness that Angelique had forgotten for a minute there was anyone else in the room. "Don't frighten your poor brother!"

Joseph recovered quickly now that there was an ally. "Yes, it is probably after *you*. You are the one who promised Papa you would go out to the barn and see that the horses had a bit of hay before bedtime." He smiled smugly.

Angelique wished she hadn't mentioned *Wendigoes* and she wished she hadn't promised Papa. It got dark so early in the winter. It was long before suppertime and already the sky was darkening. With the snow whipping around the house, she had better hurry and go out while she could still see. She pulled up her hood and wrapped her scarf around her face.

The screeching of the wind seemed to increase as she opened the door and slipped out into the cold. For a moment she stood, her back to the door. Even with her scarf on, the cold seemed to reach in and pinch her nostrils so that she couldn't breathe. Angelique pushed herself away from the shelter of the doorway.

In the dim daylight, the barn was almost lost in the swirl of snow. It was not much of a barn. It had begun as a log lean-to between the pasture and the corral, but Papa had closed it in for the winter so that on stormy days the horses would have shelter. It took all of Angelique's strength to push open the heavy door far enough to slip inside. It was a relief to be in, though it was even darker and gloomier inside and the shrieking of the wind seemed to be magnified by the holes between the logs in the roof.

She would have been frightened again by imaginary creatures were it not for the welcoming snorts and nickering of the horses. Gurnuy was closest. He swung away from the manger where he was tied and pushed his rump against Angelique, shoving her against the wall. She wasn't very fond of her brother's pony, but she gave him a welcoming pat as she pushed him away. At least coping with him took her mind away from scary things. She smiled at the rough winter coats the horses grew, so different from the sleek look they had in summer. *Gurnuy looks a little like a tousled bear,* she thought as she slipped behind the manger, grabbed an armful of hay, and dropped some in front of each horse tied there. There was one other beside Gurnuy.

La Griz was a rangy grey mare Papa had got to replace Michif as his buffalo runner. Papa was training her and Angelique could only hope that the horse would carry Papa safely in the spring hunt. In her opinion the mare would never be half the horse Michif had been. She knew it wasn't La Griz's fault, but Angelique had not been able to bring herself to befriend the mare.

They had a third horse: Mennwi. Papa had taken him to pull the sleigh when he drove Maman to the LaVallées' house. Angelique was definitely friends with him ever since she'd ridden him to get help for Maman. She knew that one reason Papa had bought Mennwi from their neighbour was to help Angelique carry on without her beloved Michif. Her eyes welled with tears at the memory of the gallant pinto horse.

The barn door was even harder to tug shut as she left, but she managed even as the wind whipped at her and the snow stung the bits of her face that weren't covered by her scarf. It would not take long to freeze in this weather. But she wouldn't go back to the house. Not yet.

She slid her mittened hand along the icy logs of the corral until she came to a corner behind the barn. There, in a little space where the logs jutted out and made a sort of alcove, hung a bridle. Michif's bridle. It had been kind of Papa to give it to her. Even though the homemade leather it was fashioned from was very worn, it could have been used on another horse. He hadn't done that; he'd let her keep it as a memento and she'd hung it here.

Before the snow had come she'd hung flowers around it; it still had the remnants of a little wreath of *kinik-kinik* that she'd woven. Most of the shiny leaves were gone now. She decided that when the storm was over, she would try to get down to the little spruce trees along the river and make a winter wreath.

Was it her imagination again or was it really much warmer as she stood here? True, she was out of the path of the wind, but this special corner felt safe. No *Wendigo* could harm her here. She could almost smell the sharp odour of Michif when she'd ridden him across the prairie.

She had heard her father and mother talking about what Papa called "Michif's shrine." And she knew Maman worried that her daughter was making "too much of a horse." But Papa shook his head. "Let her have her 'Saint Michif' for a while if it helps her," he'd said. "She's mourning for a lost friend."

Angelique turned back into the wrath of the wind. It was getting dark and she'd better get back to the house while she could still find it in the thickening snow. She'd been gone a long time, and she didn't want Joseph deciding that he should come to her rescue the way he had when they'd been kidnapped by the horse raiders. The last thing she needed was a brave but foolish little brother wandering around lost in the storm.

CHAPTER No. 2

Angelique lay snuggled under her quilt that night, reaching her toes down to the warmth of the stone she'd heated and wrapped in an old shirt of Papa's. She'd done one for Joseph's cot too and had carefully moved it down the bedding to where his feet would be so that the whole bed would be warm when he climbed in. She and Thérèse had built up the fire so that there would be some heat during the night. One of them would get up and put more wood on when the cabin started to cool. That was usually Papa's job but he had not returned.

He had taken Maman to stay with the LaVallées now that it was nearly time for the *bebé* to be born. Madame LaVallée helped most of the women who were having *bebés*. Angelique was relieved that Maman would be there being cared for, but she missed her already. She was glad though that Papa had not attempted to come home through the storm. He would know that they would be fine. There was plenty of wood in the woodbox. If they needed more, the stack that Papa and Joseph had made along the side of the cabin would be easy to find, even if it was covered with snow.

From the bed across from her, her cousin, Thérèse, blew out the candle.

"Bonswer," Angelique murmured.

Thérèse's *"bonsoir"* was muffled as though her face was buried in her pillow.

Angelique's heart felt a twitch of sorrow. Thérèse was crying. Again. So many nights since Thérèse had come to live with them Angelique had wakened to hear a gentle sobbing in the room they shared. Thérèse's young husband, Alphonse, had been killed on the fall hunt, just as Michif had.

In a way Maman's difficult pregnancy had been a blessing. Angelique and Thérèse had to look after her. For Angelique, at least, the thought of the *bebé* had been a bright spot that had helped her get through the pain of losing Michif. She was sure the *bebé* was a girl—a sister.

It seemed to Angelique that she had hardly closed her eyes when she was wakened by Joseph. She could barely see him in the dark by her bed but she felt him shaking her.

"What's wrong?" she murmured. *"Kikwaay ispayin?"*

"Angelique," he whispered, his mouth close to her ear, "I'm afraid!"

"Nothing to be afraid of," Angelique mumbled. "Go back to bed."

"I'm alone out there," Joseph was whimpering in her ear now. "Papa's not home … and … and there's the *Wendigo*!"

Angelique groaned to herself. There was no help for it. Joseph was as stubborn as a mule. He wouldn't go away and he wouldn't let her be. As much as she hated to leave the cozy warmth of her cot, she'd have to humour him.

"All right," she whispered, climbing out of bed. "Help me move my bed into the front room."

She could see better now in the flickering light from the fire. They'd left the blanket that usually covered the doorway to her little bedroom pulled back to let in heat.

Joseph was pushing on her cot almost before she was out of it. It slid easily over the floor. Joseph was definitely strong for a seven-year-old. Angelique scrambled to move Maman's braided-rag mats out of the way.

Mercifully, they didn't waken Thérèse.

They pushed Angelique's cot alongside Joseph's, near the fire.

"Get into bed *vite*. Go quick before your feet freeze right off," she commanded. Angelique's feet were freezing already, and Joseph had been out of bed longer than she had. She hastened to slip a few pieces of wood onto the fire. Two chopped ones went on the coals and then a larger uncut log on top. That would burn longer and keep the fire going. Grateful that there was still some warmth at the foot of her bed, she scrambled in.

"Bonswer," she mumbled.

The wind still howled outside, but the crackle of the newly burning sticks in the fire was comforting. She closed her eyes and snuggled down to go back to sleep.

"Angelique?" Joseph evidently had other plans. "There isn't really a *Wendigo,* is there?"

She didn't answer. Let him think she was asleep.

"Is there, Angelique? Angelique?" He waited a moment and then louder, "Angelique!"

Whatever made her think she could ignore Joseph and he would give up? Ignoring him only made him more persistent. Any louder and he'd wake poor Thérèse. Angelique didn't want her crying again. Let her have some peace.

"No!" she said impatiently. "There is no *Wendigo*!" She was tired but she wasn't about to let Joseph get off so easily. "But there is a bogeyman! Mrs. Ross says so."

"Then he'll get you for trying to scare me!" Joseph seemed to have recovered some spirit.

This could lead to having him awake half the night. "Fine," she grumbled. "I'll take care of the bogeyman *and* the *Wendigo* … you go to sleep!"

For a little while she thought he might have. No such luck.

"Angelique …," his voice was softer now, sleepy but worried, "Maman will be all right, won't she?"

"Of course. Madame LaVallée knows all about helping mothers have *bebés*." Now she was trying to convince herself as well as Joseph. "Maman will be home in a few days with a beautiful *bebé* for us to love." It was useless to try to get Joseph to settle down while his mind was on things that worried him. And she herself was wide awake now too.

"Look!" she said. "See the beautiful patterns the firelight makes on the wall." Golden shadows lit the room.

"Ummm," Joseph murmured. "They're dancing like *lii chiran*. Before, I thought the flickering was the *Wendigo* creeping in."

Good, thought Angelique, *he's settling down.* "You know," she said, "sometimes when you are warm and cozy in your bed, having the wind howl outside just makes you feel cozier." She wanted to add "now go to sleep" but didn't dare. She hoped he would watch the dancing firelight that reminded him of the Northern Lights and doze off.

It worked. But long after Joseph had gone to sleep and the flames had ceased to flicker, leaving the room lit only by a soft glow, it was Angelique who lay awake, wondering about Maman.

In the morning, with the fire built up and the smell of their breakfast of tea and bannock, Joseph was his old self. Unfortunately. He'd already upset one cup of tea while trying to hide Angelique's cup as Thérèse was setting the table.

Around the window the frost-covered nails stood out like fuzzy white caterpillars. Joseph tried to melt one with his finger, but it wouldn't melt down to the nail and instead left an ugly ice-covered nail head.

It was hopeless to try to look out the window, but Angelique thought the frost designs were beautiful—like some rich, white tapestry of ferns and jungle patterns, except for the little circle Joseph had scratched trying to see out.

"The storm is over," said Thérèse pouring more tea.

It saddened Angelique to see the dark circles under her cousin's eyes. "Yes," she said cheerfully, "Papa will be coming home." And to her brother, "Joseph! Not so much *siru d'pwer* on the bannock. Thérèse and I want some too!"

Joseph ignored her, of course. "We can go out and feed the horses together … good to have chores done before Papa comes home." He sounded smug at having thought of it.

He was right but Angelique wasn't about to say so. They left the dishwashing to Thérèse. They would bring her a couple of pails of snow to melt for the dishwater.

Angelique couldn't wait to get outside.

It was still cold but the world had been swept clean by the storm, and drifted snow was piled high against the fences. They would be able to dig tunnels to play in. Joseph was testing a huge drift at the corral by walking on it right to the top of the rails. They would be able to tunnel under that one and make a little playhouse with rooms for each of them.

"Come on, Joseph!" she was running toward a smooth white slope of fresh snow. "Let's make angels!"

When their father arrived, they were still at it, lying in the snow swinging their arms and legs, making the patterns over and over. Joseph ruined his angel by jumping up and running through the snow to Papa, but Angelique stood carefully and jumped out so as to keep the angel perfect. She even made a halo on top with her finger.

"How is Maman?" she asked Papa breathlessly as he climbed from the sleigh.

"She is okay." He gave them each a hug. "And … so is your baby sister!"

Angelique's heart felt as if it would burst. "The *bebé* is here!" She danced around Papa. A girl! She couldn't wait to see her *bebé*. The little sister she and Maman had hoped for. It was wonderful. She would cover the hillside with angels.

"Angelique!" Joseph had taken the news happily but obviously wasn't as thrilled that the baby was a girl. "We forgot to feed the horses for Papa!"

But even that could not cloud her day. Papa didn't seem to care. "It's all right," he said. "The day is fine and they can be out in the pasture and dig for grass. I'll water them first and you can give Mennwi some hay before he joins them." He turned to unhitch the horse. Angelique hurried over to stroke the shaggy black head and hold the horse while Joseph unhooked the traces.

"Enn pchit fiiy!" she whispered to the horse. It was true—it had really happened. But telling Mennwi made her remember how she had first whispered the secret to Michif. How could she have forgotten him just now? After she made the angels, she would go down to the river and find a spruce tree to make that wreath.

Joseph ruined his angel by jumping up and running through the snow to Papa, but Angelique stood carefully and jumped out so as to keep the angel perfect.

"When will Maman be able to come home?" Joseph was impatient. "Will it be soon? When can we see the *bebé*?" And without waiting for an answer he began to laugh. "Does she have buffalo eyes like Angelique?"

Angelique pretended she hadn't heard the last bit. It had been ages since Joseph had called her that. She started to lead Mennwi to the barn but slowly so that she could hear Papa's reply.

"I'm sure she will have beautiful brown eyes … just like Angelique!" Papa laughed. "And we can go and see Maman and the *bebé* tomorrow … and if Madame LaVallée says it is all right we will bring them home. Now," he said taking Joseph by the hand, "do you think you could stand still while I take the broom to you and see if I can get some of that snow off? You look like a *bonnom di niizh*!"

Angelique knew she looked like a snowman too, but she didn't care. She tied Mennwi to the corral and went to fetch him a bit of hay away from the other horses so they wouldn't steal it.

It would be good to have Maman home again but she was glad they would be able to visit the LaVallées. She'd have a chance to talk to her friend, François—after she spent some time with the *bebé,* of course.

She missed François. They had been good friends but now that they were older, the others teased them if they spent any time together. "Angelique has a *jaeng*!" or "François and Angelique want to hold hands!" It made her angry but there wasn't much she could do about it. Joseph and François's younger brothers were the worst, but they could run them down and give them a snowy face wash. It was the other children at school who made it a problem. She would have put up with it, but François hated it so much that now he avoided her if there were others around.

She helped Papa and Joseph put the horses in the pasture and then ran back to the hillside. Lying in the snow making angels, breathing the sharp winter air, and looking up at the deep blue of the sky above, she could pretend she was floating up into the sky. Like an angel.

She was counting angels when Thérèse called her to come and eat. Twenty-one. Some of the small ones, she had to admit, were rather messy but it was an impressive Heavenly Host anyway. Her own special celebration. A festival of angels. If only the wind didn't drift them full of snow, she could show Maman when she came home.

"How much longer do you think I should stay?" Thérèse was asking Papa when Angelique came in the door.

Angelique knew that Thérèse had decided not to remain in Batoche but to return to Saint Boniface. She planned to visit her family and then go to stay in the convent where she'd studied before she came west to marry Alphonse.

Angelique had heard her telling Maman, "Perhaps if I have a vocation, the sisters will let me take the vows and become a nun too."

And Maman had been cautious. "That is a big decision to make. Wait, Thérèse, until your heart has healed a bit. Besides," she had smiled, "you might find yourself with other things you need to do."

Angelique watched her cousin ladling out the bowls of soup and cutting thick slices of bread for everyone. In the black dress of mourning that Thérèse wore every day, she looked as if she were already a nun. At least the way Angelique thought they looked. She had never seen one herself.

Papa took his time answering. "I hope you will wait and see. Surely you will not wish to travel such a long way until winter is over?"

Thérèse nodded sadly. "No," she said, "I hadn't thought of that."

Angelique had not understood before how sad this place must be for her cousin. After all this was where, in the space of a little over a month, she had married and buried a loving young husband. Something should be said to distract her before she began crying again.

"Thérèse," Angelique said in her most cheerful voice. "After we eat would you come for a walk with me?"

She rushed on before her cousin could refuse. "I want to go down the bank to the river and see if I can find the spruce trees." She kept going. "You should see how lovely the trees look now … all covered with frost … and the drifts look like waves from the sea." Angelique stopped. She'd never seen sea waves either. "At least I think that's how they'd look." She was embarrassed now.

But she made her cousin smile at her enthusiasm. Thérèse gave Angelique's shoulder a pat and said softly, "Perhaps that would be a very good idea. As soon as we have our tea, we will wash up and go."

Papa and Joseph were hauling manure from the little barn as they went by, and Angelique took great pleasure in waving as she and Thérèse began their walk. She hoped that Joseph noticed that while he still had to work, she was free as a bird. It seemed though that he didn't care. The silly boy was just happy to be doing "men's work" with Papa. Still, nothing could ruin her good mood, and she smiled with delight when

Thérèse saw the multitude of angels and pronounced them *"splendide."*

It was slow walking. In some places the wind had swept the riverbank bare and slippery, but once they came to the bushes, the drifts were very deep and they had to lift their moccasined feet high while their skirts dragged in the snow. Sometimes, where the drifts had packed the snow firm, they could walk right on top, the way Joseph had done at the corral. But always, eventually, they would break through and fall laughing in the snow.

It was good, Angelique decided, to see Thérèse laughing for a change. And the fresh air had lessened the pallor of her cheeks. She looked a bit more like the lovely young bride she'd been only last fall instead of the haggard widow she'd become.

"Wait there, Thérèse!" Angelique cried as she headed for a particularly high drift ahead of them. "I'll test this one and see if it will hold us!"

The snow was packed firm. Angelique climbed higher and higher and the drift held. "Look at me!" She turned to call back to Thérèse, took one more step, and disappeared completely.

"Angelique!" Thérèse screamed. "Are you all right?"

Angelique had snow in her mouth, her eyes, her hair, and it took her a minute to answer. "I'm fine," she called.

Looking straight up she could see the sky but to all sides of her there was nothing but snow. To make matters worse, beneath all that snow the bank was steep here. Her feet in their slippery moccasins slid out from under her. Now she was covered in snow and the snow above was dropping down on her.

Quickly she scrambled back to where she had fallen through, relieved that she could see the sky again and didn't feel so trapped.

"I'm coming," called Thérèse.

Angelique had a mouthful of snow and couldn't answer right away. "Don't try to walk on top," she called when she could speak again. "You'll break through too!"

"You're right," Thérèse's voice seemed a little nearer but muffled by the snow between them. "I shall just try to stomp down the snow and clear a path." Thérèse sounded worried. "Perhaps I should get your Papa to come and help!"

"Let us try first to get to each other!" Angelique could just imagine Joseph telling everyone about it. "Angelique got buried in the snowbank," he would say, "and we had to dig her out like *enn patak*!"

She was kicking at the snow now, wishing she had Father Moulin's hard boots instead of her soft moccasins. But she'd uncovered a broken bit of branch and with that she could loosen the snow and then scoop it away. Now she could tunnel her way back up the bank toward Thérèse.

"Keep talking, Thérèse," she called, "so I'll know where you are!"

She could hear that Thérèse sounded puzzled. "Where are you Angelique? You sound closer but I can't see you at all!"

Angelique smiled and dug faster. This was really rather fun, now that she wasn't afraid of being lost. The snow above her as she tunnelled along seemed firm enough and she was moving quite quickly, loosening the snow with the branch, then scooping it away and moving into the new space. She had just scooped out another batch when the bank in front of her collapsed and she was facing a pair of moccasins stomping the snow. She crawled out and looked up at Thérèse's shocked face.

"I'm a pretty good badger, *non*?" She laughed.

Thérèse was laughing too but not for long. "You're covered with snow and you'll be frozen if we don't get you home soon. Come on!" She grabbed Angelique's hand and began pulling her back the way they had come.

It was true. Angelique had been sheltered by the snow tunnel and the digging had kept her warm. Now she could feel the chill of the day. Even her toes, wrapped in pieces of blanket inside the moccasins, were feeling cool. The cousins hurried back to the cabin.

"Angelique!" Joseph called as they walked quickly past the barn and corral. "You look like *en zweezuu d'niizh*!" He was running toward them. "A snowbird with buffalo eyes, of course!"

"He thinks he is sooo funny," Angelique mumbled as Thérèse brought out the broom and began to sweep the snow off her cousin. Snow clung to every bit of her. Where her hair hung down beneath her hood, it seemed to be more like brown icicles than hair.

"What you need now, *ma fille,* is some dry clothes and hot tea to warm you up," said Thérèse.

"You're going in?" Joseph said looking surprised. "Aren't we going to dig tunnels?"

Angelique knew he was disappointed but she didn't care. "I don't feel like it any more!" she said, following Thérèse indoors.

CHAPTER No 4

*The LaVallée house seemed to be wall-to-*wall children. In the summer most of them would be playing or working outside. But every time Angelique came to visit in the winter, she wondered how they all fit in.

"Entrez! Entrez!" Madame LaVallée welcomed them at the door, pulling them inside as if she had been longing for four more people to add to the crowded front room.

Angelique squeezed past her and rushed over to where Maman was lying on a cot in the corner of the room. Above her, within easy reach, hung a tiny blanket hammock. After she'd hugged her children Maman reached up and removed the *bebé*.

Like picking a berry from a bush, Angelique smiled. What a sweet berry! The bright eyes looked straight at her. *She knows that I am her sister.* Once again Angelique felt she'd float away with joy.

Then Joseph spoiled the moment, of course, pushing his face in the way. Instantly the *bebé's* tiny face crumpled and she began to cry. A very small cry, Angelique thought. She resisted the temptation to give Joseph a shove. It would be just like him to fall on the *bebé*.

Her forbearance was rewarded.

"Would you like to hold her, Angelique?" Maman asked. "Just for a moment until I can feed her?"

Angelique couldn't speak. She nodded happily as the amazing wee bundle was placed in her arms. True, the *bebé* was still crying. No doubt she was still alarmed by Joseph. But it was not a sad sound—almost funny, Angelique thought, a little like a calf calling for its mother in the Vennes' pasture. Besides, compared with all the hubbub from the LaVallée young ones, the *bebé* seemed very quiet indeed.

For a while after Maman took the *bebé* to nurse, Angelique sat on the floor beside the cot. She was marvelling at a tiny hand with its perfect fingers. It was amazing the fingernails could be so small yet so perfect. And when she reached up to touch the *bebé's* hand, it curled around her finger and held on tight. *She knows,* Angelique thought, *that I love her and will look after her.*

Papa was there now looking both proud and concerned. "Will you be able to come home soon?"

Angelique realized she had not really looked at her mother. Even with the hug, her eyes had been on the bundle in the blanket above. Now she did look and was shocked at how pale Maman was. *She's just tired,* Angelique told herself. Everyone said having a *bebé* was hard work. But her heart sank as she realized that it meant Maman would not be coming home today. And neither would the *bebé*.

"Not yet, Louise," Maman was smiling but her eyes were filled with tears. Angelique was afraid that she would start crying too.

Luckily Madame LaVallée had bustled over with tea. Somehow she found a spot for Maman's cup beside the cot and even had managed to clear some space on the table where François and his brothers were playing cards.

"Go help Madame, Angelique," Maman whispered. "You can hold the *bebé* again when I've finished nursing."

Reluctantly Angelique peeled the *bebé's* fingers away. Maman was right, she should be helping. She could see Thérèse bringing bowls to the table.

"François, you and your brothers will have to play in the loft until after we've eaten." Madame LaVallée shooed the boys away from the table. Already one of the younger boys was scrambling up the ladder to where Monsieur LaVallée had made them a room. A very practical solution. The loft was warm from the heat rising from the fire, though Angelique wondered how any of them ever settled down to sleep at night.

She was sure the *bebé* would be much better off at home in her bedroom where it was quiet. *If only Maman was strong enough to travel,* she thought as she and Thérèse arranged the bowls and spoons and Madame LaVallée brought a huge pot of soup. Angelique could see the *glissantes* floating in it and realized she was very hungry. Now she hoped that Maman would not finish feeding the *bebé* before she could have at least one of those fluffy dumplings and sip some of the soup. *Yes,* she thought as she began to eat the soup, *it is every bit as delicious as it looks.*

"So Marguerite … Louise …," Madame LaVallée smiled. "Have you thought of a name for the little one yet?"

Angelique was shocked. How could she have missed that? She couldn't keep calling her little sister *"bebé"* forever. Names were so important. Maman was holding the *bebé* out to her. "Do you have any ideas, Angelique?"

Angelique finished her meal and went to hold the little one. No crying now. The little rosebud lips were closed, the translucent eyelids with their tiny lashes too. "She is like a rosebud."

Papa laughed. "She won't always be a bud. Someday she'll be a rose. Why not call her Rose?"

"Was there a Saint Rose?" Madame LaVallée was up again bringing more tea. "We must ask Father Moulin when he comes to see Marguerite."

"We will give her a saint's name too." Papa was looking at Maman. "We can call her Marguerite for the saint and you."

Angelique glanced up from the *bebé's* perfect wee face. Papa was looking sad, she thought. He should be happy to have such a perfect baby daughter. "We can call her *Pchit* Rose for now," she said. She bent to kiss the tiny forehead and caught the sharp clean smell of the newborn. She supposed Papa was sad as he would not be able to take Maman and *Pchit* Rose home today.

She realized as they were leaving that she hadn't spent any time with François at all. He seemed to understand though. He went to help Papa and Monsieur LaVallée harness Mennwi to the sleigh. She and Joseph stayed with Maman and *Pchit* Rose as long as they could.

"Rest and get strong so you can come home, Maman," she whispered.

It wasn't until later, huddled beneath the buffalo robes in the sleigh, that she wondered about Père Moulin's visit. Surely it was just a visit. Maman was just tired. Wasn't she?

CHAPTER No 5

Each day Papa would hitch Mennwi to the sleigh and go to visit Maman and *Pchit* Rose. Each day he came back without them. Each day, he looked weary and anxious.

Angelique and Joseph took turns going along. Maman seemed to tire easily. Today was Joseph's turn and Thérèse had gone too, but Angelique didn't mind. It was a beautiful afternoon and François had ridden Pisiskees over to visit.

Angelique thought she could taste the sunshine as it glistened on the snow. On the hillside her celebration of angels glistened and shone. The wind had not been strong enough to drift over them yet.

"Come on, François!" She ran ahead of him toward the riverbank. "I'll show you my tunnel!"

The sun had warmed and melted the top of the snowdrifts, making a firm crust. The drifted snow above the tunnel was still solid. They crawled through. It surprised Angelique to see how far she had actually dug.

"And here," she announced standing up and pointing to the opening above, "is where I disappeared!" She could tell François was impressed at how deep the snow was as he looked up through it to the sky above. There was barely room for the two of them to stand there. "And here," she said pointing down, "is where I fell down and slid away!"

Maybe it was because it was so crowded that she had to move over to give him room or maybe it was because her moccasined feet happened to be in the same icy spot as before, but she'd no sooner spoken than her feet slipped out from under her and she was sliding down the icy hill-side. This time she didn't stop but plowed into the snow on the steep bank and kept going.

"Collinn!" she shrieked.

At last she burst through the snow on the bank. But it was too steep and slippery to stop. She kept sliding until the bank flattened out. Close below her was the frozen river. She could hear François let out a whoop as he slid through.

"Look out!"

She jumped out of the way just in time as he came sliding down. He ended up even closer to the river.

François picked himself up and beamed. "Angelique! You clever one! You have made us a wonderful *chute*. We can slide better than otters on this!" He turned back toward the slide.

Angelique watched him. It was true. It was a wonderful slide and the more they used it, the more polished the icy surface would become and the faster they would go.

There was just one problem. She waited until she could see that François had noticed it too.

There was no way to get back up. They stood looking at each other. Neither said a word.

In the summer there was a narrow path down the riverbank behind Angelique's home. It was very steep until it came to the level bit by the river. Joseph and Angelique sometimes scrambled down, laughing and falling until they reached the little clearing by the river. Sometimes they would bring a *picnique* and eat beside the water.

When she and Maman had come in the fall, they had stayed up above. The path had been dry but Maman had not wanted to risk being unable to climb back up.

In the spring, the bank was muddy and slippery and they slid down like otters, while Papa or Maman called to be careful. Then she and Joseph had to hold onto the bushes beside the path, sometimes grabbing a low-hanging tree branch to pull themselves back up.

Now those trees and bushes were deep in snow. Most of the bushes hardly showed above the snowbanks. The path had become the icy slide. François was trying to scramble up the open part but he wasn't making much progress. Angelique knew that once he got into the tunnel, it was even steeper. And icier.

"I don't think that will work!" she called. He backed up and took a run at it. For every three steps he scrambled up he slid back two until, after running frantically in the same place, he skidded back to the bottom and collapsed in the snow.

"Do you still think I've discovered a wonderful slide?" She couldn't resist teasing him a little.

"It will be *fantastique* … if we ever manage to get back to the top," he laughed.

She was glad he was still in a good mood.

They tried pushing each other up, but although one of them then managed to get farther up, it wasn't far enough. They ended up collapsed in a heap at the bottom.

They tried bringing some long branches they were able to dig out of the snow and using them to hold onto. But the branches would slide away and they didn't get very far that way either.

"We could wait for your father to come home," François suggested at last as they stood staring up the bank. "He could let a rope down the tunnel and pull us up."

Angelique doubted that there was a piece of rope in Batoche long enough unless they pulled down the ferry cable, and they couldn't do that. She shook her head. "That could be nearly dark … we've got to think of something before that."

Though neither of them spoke, they both turned and looked at the river. It was hopeless to try to walk along the banks. The bushes came all the way down in most places and the snow was deep. It would take forever to try to crawl and dig their way along. But the river would be easy walking.

With all the cold weather it should be frozen solid. The ice would eventually be a couple of feet thick.

"There are sleighs coming across at the ferry crossing now," François said tentatively.

Angelique looked at him. They had both been forbidden to go on the river ice even with an adult.

"We wouldn't have to go all the way down to the ferry … we could walk on the river to our place. It's less than a mile." He was being very persuasive. "Papa keeps the track down cleared and it's not as steep as it is here …"

His voice trailed off and he looked at Angelique expectantly.

Neither of them said anything as they turned and walked to the edge. They both knew that sometimes there were air pockets along the shore where the ice would be thin, places where the current eddied and kept the ice only a few inches thick long after the rest was frozen solid.

François stopped and looked at her. "I could go alone and send someone back for you …"

Angelique gave him a look. This was no time for foolish bravery. "And what if you go through the ice and don't make it?" she said sweetly. "I suppose I should just stay here and freeze to death?"

François laughed. "We'll each drag one of those long branches along," he said picking the heaviest, "so if one of us falls in, the other can fish the wet one out!"

Angelique nodded and picked up the other branch. She didn't like to imagine what it would be like once you were fished out of the icy water and had nearly a mile to walk, even on a sunny day like this. But she didn't say a word as François led the way onto the ice.

CHAPTER No. 6

"I'll go first," François said. "You follow a little distance behind. That way it won't be as heavy as if we were side by side."

Angelique nodded. She watched as he stepped carefully out onto the river and then she followed in his tracks.

They stayed away from the shore, where the ice would be thin because of the air pockets. Once, when François moved closer to the bank, there was an ominous cracking sound. Angelique swung her branch over toward him so quickly she almost knocked him over! He grabbed it and came back to where she was.

"Too close, I guess," he said.

Walking on the river was not always easy. In places the snow was piled deep, while in others the ice had been smoothed and polished by the wind. Angelique decided she liked the snowy bits best; her moccasins slipped and skidded when on the smooth surface but that was not what bothered her. Somehow the opaque ice below reminded her that she was walking on the river. Then she could imagine that it was water and she would be trying to walk on it and falling in. Better to just pretend she was on solid ground and enjoy the walk.

The sun still shone but the shadows were lengthening. She told herself it was good that they had decided to come this way. Once the sun began to go down, it would quickly get cold.

"We're here!" François called back to her.

She looked up to see the cleared bank he had promised sloping up to the LaVallées' house. Even better, she could see their sleigh sitting out in front, Mennwi pawing the snow impatiently.

"They are still there!" She began to run as François turned toward the shore.

"Stay back!" he warned. "The ice won't be thick here. Papa kept a place chopped open for a while so the horses could drink." He stood staring at the shore. "I've got to remember exactly where it was … the snow has covered it so it all looks the same."

Angelique stopped in her tracks. *Wonderful,* she thought, *we've come all this way and we'll probably fall through here.* She could almost feel the ice beneath her feet parting as it cracked under her—then the sensation of freezing cold waters closing over her head as she sank to the bottom.

"At least it won't be deep if we do go through!" He was still standing staring at the shoreline. "It was only up to the horses' knees when they went in to drink."

Angelique began to revise her imaginary descent to the depths of the river. This time the icy water came to her knees. Then she began to laugh. She'd been "borrowing sorrow" again.

That's what her mother called it when she let her imagination run away with her.

"I'm glad you are amused," François turned to look at her. "I am about to risk a fall into the river to get us safely to shore, you know!" He was trying to look stern but Angelique could see he was holding back a grin. "Here I go."

Angelique pulled her stick so that it stood upright. "And I am ready to save you!" she called. She was sure by the confident way he was walking that he'd remembered exactly where the hole had been.

"All right, you can follow in my footprints," he called as he jumped onto the bank. But then his arms started to windmill and he lost his balance and fell back onto the snowy ice.

Angelique watched in dismay. He'd landed hard. Would the ice break? She moved slowly toward him, pushing her stick ahead. His arms were still moving. He hadn't gone through; why was he trying to swim? She watched as he stood up and inched ashore.

"There you are," he said pointing to where he'd fallen. "Another snow angel for Angelique!"

She was laughing as she ran toward the shore. Not wanting to spoil the angel she veered over.

"No, Angelique! Not there!" François was yelling.

She was running. She could stop but could she stop quickly enough? She had no doubt from the look on François's face that she'd run onto the part where the ice would be thin, but she was close to the bank now. Another few feet and she'd be there. There was the ominous cracking sound all around her as she jumped.

She'd have lost her balance and fallen backward the way François had if he hadn't grabbed her hand and yanked her hard farther up onto the bank.

She lay there face down in the snow. *"Maarsi,"* she said spitting out a mouthful of snow as she stood up. "You didn't have to rescue me quite that hard!" But she smiled at him so he'd know she wasn't really angry. He was a good friend and

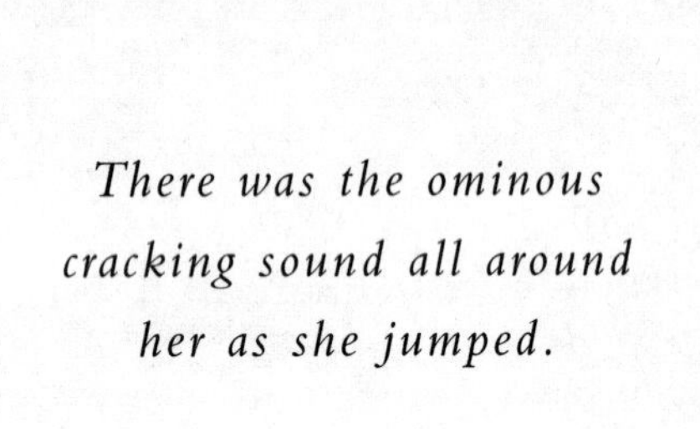

There was the ominous cracking sound all around her as she jumped.

just the person she'd want to have around for an adventure.

François was looking up the bank toward the house. "Isn't that Father Moulin's cabriolet?"

Angelique looked too. It was the fancy sleigh Father always drove. Had it been there before? It could have been; it was farther back than theirs was, and she might not have seen it from out on the river. Why was Father Moulin there? He didn't often visit people—he only came when someone was sick or dying, and this was the second time he'd come to visit Maman and the *bebé*.

Angelique began to run. She was out of breath when she reached the yard.

Joseph was standing outside the door crying.

CHAPTER No 7

"What's wrong?" Angelique was almost screaming.

Joseph just stood there, his face screwed up.

"Is it Maman? The *bebé*?" She grabbed him and began to shake him by the shoulders.

He wrestled free and gave her an angry look. "Now you've given me the hiccups!" he sobbed.

"What happened?" François was there now and Joseph seemed to respond better to his calm voice.

"I got into a fight with Pierre … and Papa has banished me!" He was trying not to cry now. Angelique knew that he hated to be caught crying but would let himself be a little boy when he thought no one would see.

"Oh, Joseph …"

She felt like shaking him even more for scaring her, but she knew it wasn't his fault. She'd been "borrowing sorrow" again. It wasn't unusual for him and François's younger brother to get into a tussle, though most of the time they were the best of friends.

He was rubbing at his eyes with his fists. Suddenly he looked at her. "What are you doing here?" he demanded. "Aren't you supposed to be at home?" Then he looked even more puzzled. "And why did you come from down by the river?" Suddenly he was all curiosity, as if he had never been crying at all.

"It's a long story," François said. "We sort of got stranded and had to come along the river …"

"You walked on the ice?" Joseph's face lit up. "Oh, Angelique!" He turned and ran to the house. "You are going to be in such big trouble!"

Angelique and François looked at each other

and began to follow slowly. "Better me than him," she said. "It doesn't take much to cheer my brother up!"

They followed Joseph inside. The usual noise of children playing and adults talking greeted them. At least the adults ceased talking when they arrived. Angelique wondered if anything would silence the children completely.

Maman was sitting up. Angelique thought she looked better, much better.

Angelique slipped out of her coat and hurried over to Maman. Where was the *bebé*? The blanket hung empty above. Once again Angelique almost panicked. She caught herself in time. Maman, she realized, would hardly be sitting smiling as she sipped her tea if anything had happened to *Pchit* Rose.

Maman wasn't just smiling, she was laughing. "Angelique, *ma belle,* you should see your face!" She pointed to the other side of the room. "Thérèse is holding Rose for me!"

Angelique turned. The LaVallée parents and

Papa were at the door saying goodbye to Père Moulin, and she supposed she should at least have said *"bonjour,"* but he didn't seem to have noticed her. Besides, she'd been too worried about Maman and *Pchit* Rose.

Joseph was standing next to Papa, looking as if he would burst. Somehow he restrained himself from saying anything while the priest was there. Angelique supposed she should be grateful for that, but there'd be no stopping her brother once the door closed.

Madame LaVallée beat him to it. "Did you and Angelique ride Pisiskees here?" she asked.

"No!" Joseph was almost bouncing with excitement. "They came by the river … they walked on the ice!"

That silenced the room. Even the LaVallée children stared wide-eyed at the news. Maman looked at Angelique, her face changing from shock to disappointment.

Angelique took a deep breath and began to explain.

CHAPTER No. 8

Angelique thought the ordeal of telling why they had come along the river ice was much more frightening than the actual trip. She was glad it was over. It had taken a lot of explaining why they had done something that was strictly forbidden, but they weren't going to be punished.

Secretly Angelique thought it was because she and François had proved themselves to be very resourceful when they had survived being kidnapped after the spring hunt.

And, of course, neither of them said a word about the ice cracking.

It would take more than a scolding to dim her joy at knowing her baby sister and Maman would be home at last. Not today but first thing tomorrow, Papa would be coming to get them.

For now, François would be coming home with them so that he could ride his pony back home in the morning. So the sleigh was full with the three children in the back and Thérèse riding with Papa in front.

Joseph sat beside her looking like a storm cloud. The only bright spot she'd had during the questioning at the LaVallées' house had been seeing Joseph's face go from triumph to puzzlement to disappointment when he saw that she wasn't in as much trouble as he'd hoped. She beamed over at Joseph now.

It was late by the time they settled in to bed. Joseph had cheered up noticeably when he realized that François would be sleeping in the front room with him. He was sure François was much better protection from bogeymen and *Wendigoes* than Angelique could possibly be.

It wasn't until nearly dawn that Angelique woke to the shrill cry. She was almost out of bed ready to run to the *bebé* when she realized it was the sound of the wind shrieking around the house.

If the storm was as bad as the last one, Papa would not want to risk taking Maman and *Pchit* Rose out in it. Angelique felt crushed. They wouldn't be coming home today.

Obviously, François wouldn't be going home either.

Angelique shivered when her feet hit the icy floor. Since she was awake, she would just go and check the fire. She glanced over at Thérèse's bed to make sure she wouldn't waken. There was no one there. How could that be? Thérèse would never get up to stoke the fire when Papa was home. Angelique didn't need to either probably, but it wouldn't hurt to check.

She went into the front room. The fire had burned down but a soft golden glow warmed the log walls. The boys slept peacefully on either side of the fire, but there was no sign of her cousin.

She looked at the wooden pegs by the door where their coats hung. Thérèse's was gone. She rushed to pull aside the blanket that closed off Maman and Papa's room and then spun back to stare at the blank space on the wall. The peg that usually held Papa's coat was empty too. Somehow they had left without wakening anyone. Why?

She knew before looking that there would be no one in her parents' bed, but she looked anyway. Empty. Now she was not only puzzled but also worried. Papa should have wakened her and told her what was happening. Even if he expected to be back before she woke up in the morning, he would have left a note.

A note. Of course—there was her old school slate propped up against the teapot. In the dim light she could just make out Thérèse's careful handwriting, though she couldn't read what it said. She was tempted to light a candle but since the boys had managed to sleep through everything, she thought she would wait. Holding the slate very close to the fire she read: *I am very ill. We have gone to see Madame LaVallée. Your Papa will be back in the morning. Thérèse.*

Angelique felt a tinge of guilt. Perhaps Thérèse had been ill, not just unhappy. Was that why her cousin had been so pale and quiet? She decided she would put a log on the coals before she went back to bed. It must have been too much noise, for when she turned François was sitting up looking around.

"Did you know they had gone?" Angelique whispered.

François nodded. "I woke up as they were going out the door," he whispered back. He stopped and stared toward the frost-covered window.

There had been a momentary lull in the wind, but now it was back in full frenzy. It screamed around the house like a demonic chorus. Angelique thought it sounded worse than any *Wendigo*.

"When did that start?" François looked alarmed. "The weather was fine when they left."

Angelique was huddled next to the fire. She was tempted to throw open the door and show him how "fine" it was, but her feet were cold enough so she stayed where she was.

"I don't know … it woke me up just a few minutes ago."

François looked relieved. "Then they should be there by now," he said. He wasn't whispering any more. "It will probably clear up tomorrow."

Somehow he didn't sound as confident as Angelique would have liked. Winter storms were not over that quickly. The one before had lasted for a day and a night, but she had known them to go on for days.

"Well," she said, whispering again. "We have plenty of food and firewood. We'll just have to wait it out." She didn't sound as confident as she would have liked either. She was getting very cold and couldn't wait to get back to bed, though she doubted she would be able to sleep.

"Angelique!" François's head had turned to the door. "Did you hear something?"

"Wind, you mean?" She was tempted to glare at him. It wasn't like François to be silly.

"No … it sounded like a horse whinnying!" He had his head cocked to the side, listening as hard as he could.

All Angelique could hear was the shrill sound of the wind, sometimes rising to a screech, sometimes fading to a moan. "The wind sounds like a lot of things, François. It's like finding shapes in clouds. You hear a horse … I heard a baby." She turned to go back to her bedroom. Her feet really were freezing now.

"No!" François was pulling on his moccasins. "I'm sure it's a horse," he said. "I'm going to look."

Angelique ran to get dressed. She wasn't about to go outside in her nightdress. She was still convinced it was the wind, but if François was going out to check, she'd go too. She'd never get to sleep again now anyway. Perhaps he was right.

The horses might have come up from the pasture and be wanting the shelter of the barn. Perhaps they had managed to push the gate open and were outside the house. She doubted it, but she wrapped her feet in the blanket cloth, stuffed them into her moccasins, pulled them tight around her ankles, and carefully tied the leather strips. At least her feet would get warm now.

The icy blast of wind hit them the moment they opened the door. It seemed to reach into their nostrils and suck the breath from their lungs. It blew François back against her so that both of them nearly ended up back inside. Somehow they managed to get out and shut the door.

It was still dark but Angelique doubted they could have seen much in the swirling snow anyway. They'd lit the lantern using a sliver of wood to bring a flame from the coals in the fire. But even though François held it only a few feet ahead of Angelique, she could barely see the light.

Angelique looked back at the house. The little square of light from the window barely showed already. A few feet farther and there would be no sign that the house was there at all.

François was walking slowly. He had no choice. The snow had already filled in the path to the corral so that it was almost to their knees.

This was silly, Angelique thought, coming out in the blizzard to look for an imaginary horse. Even between the house and the corral and barn, they could get lost and just keep wandering in the storm. It was worse than silly—it was risking their lives.

She'd have called to François to turn back but she knew it was useless. The wind would snatch her words and carry them away. He would hear nothing but the howling as it swept the snow up and around so that it seemed to come at them from all directions. François couldn't possibly have heard a horse.

And then it was there. A furry black head shoved itself almost in her face. Mennwi. François had been right.

What was Mennwi doing here?

And then it was there.
A furry black head
shoved itself almost in
her face. Mennwi.

CHAPTER No 9

Angelique grabbed the horse's halter and started to lead him to the barn. Had Papa decided to harness La Griz and drive her to the LaVallées' place? She'd never seen the Grey One pull the sleigh. The mare was for riding and most of all to be a buffalo runner like Michif had been. Harnessing her to a sleigh seemed strange. But it made sense in a way. Mennwi had just made the trip; though it wasn't that far, perhaps Papa had decided to give him a rest.

François had moved back to Angelique and the horse. Now he brought the lantern beside

Mennwi and reached out to lift up a trace that was dragging behind.

Angelique could only stare in shock. Papa had driven Mennwi, but something had happened and he had unhitched the horse and let him go. She watched as François began to remove Mennwi's harness. Her mind was a jumble of thoughts. What could have caused Papa to let the horse go? Had the storm started that quickly? Before they had even arrived at the LaVallées' house? It seemed hard to believe. It was less than a mile. She and François had walked it the previous afternoon.

François was carrying the harness now and he moved ahead of her with the lantern. Luckily the corral came in view first. If they followed the rails, they would arrive at the little barn.

It was a struggle for the two of them to open the barn door wide enough to let Mennwi in. Angelique had to let him go to use both hands as François still held the lantern. She was sure that the horse was so anxious to get inside that he would not leave. He didn't. Unfortunately, it didn't help that he was pushing against the door, trying to get in, while she and François were doing their best to tug it open. And the wind whipped and lashed at their faces all the time.

At last they made it. Mennwi nearly knocked Angelique down as he hurried to his place at the manger. She rushed to tie him up. They would let the other horses in. François was already struggling to slide the big door that opened on the pasture. The moment it was open a few inches, horses' noses appeared, each one trying to shove the other away and be the first to get inside, out of the storm. This time at least, the eagerness to get in didn't hamper the opening of the door. Angelique helped François slide it along until it was wide enough for one horse at a time to go through.

The trouble was there were three horses trying to get in at once. La Griz was definitely biggest and strongest but Gurnuy had decided that it was ponies first and wouldn't budge. And then there was Pisiskees. Angelique could see him, though the white of him was lost in the snow; his black mane and the black raccoon rings around his eyes stood out even in the storm.

At last they got all the horses inside and managed to slide the door back. It didn't feel much warmer inside with the horses all covered in snow, but at least they were out of the wind. It was a tight squeeze with one extra horse there in the little barn, but they'd be warm. Angelique slipped behind the manger and found a bit of hay for each.

"We'd better go back to the house now," François said, "and try to figure out what to do."

Angelique just nodded. She was afraid that if she spoke, she would begin to cry. All she could think of was what could have happened to the sleigh. Where were Papa and Thérèse?

François had examined the traces on the harness when he hung it up in the barn and they did not seem to be broken. But somehow Mennwi had got away. She was glad, at least, that he'd come here; last fall he would have chosen to go back to one of his former owners and Angelique and François would never have known there'd been an accident.

Once more they struggled with the door and went out into the storm.

CHAPTER No 10

François grabbed her hand and led the way with the lantern. It was easy enough when they walked along beside the corral, but once they left that, they could see nothing.

Angelique was sure that they were headed in the right direction, but it was still dark. The wind tugged and bit at her scarf, and she could only open her eyes to narrow slits. The snow stung her eyes and face. Here in the open the storm was so strong that the wind at their sides was pushing them off course. It was as if it were trying to make them miss the house altogether. She didn't even want to move, but François was pulling her along.

The lantern hadn't gone out, but its light was so dim there was just a yellow glow around François's hand as he held the light up in front of him. Angelique wanted to tell him it wasn't worth carrying but what was the use? He wouldn't hear her anyway.

Then there was a yellow spot ahead and she realized it was the window of the house. They were so close that by the time they saw it, they had reached the door.

François opened it and the wind blew them inside.

The wrath of the storm was nothing compared with the wrath of Joseph that greeted them.

"What is the big idea?" he screamed. "Everyone goes away and leaves me alone!"

There were sobs amid the rage, and Angelique was sure that he'd been crying and terrified before they came in. Now he was relieved, she was sure, but he wasn't about to let on.

She was grateful once again to François. She was sure that no matter how much she tried to explain, Joseph would only become more furious so she said nothing.

François did not even attempt an explanation. Instead he sat down at the table facing Joseph and began to speak to him calmly.

"There is a problem, Joseph," he said carefully.

He began to explain the horse reappearing, dragging its traces. He spoke straight to Joseph, as if he hoped that if he laid the problem out clearly enough, Joseph would be able to help them think of a solution. At first Joseph still bawled with anger, but gradually his howls subsided into hiccups and he gave François his full attention.

Angelique was filled with admiration for François's tact. She decided that Joseph had calmed down enough for her to speak.

"We're afraid that the sleigh upset or got stuck in the drifts and somehow Mennwi got free and ran away home. He's still not that well broken you know," she said, remembering how she'd ridden him for help when he was only green broke. He had tried his best to buck her off. She turned to François. "When you looked at the traces in the barn, were they damaged?"

François shook his head. "Hard to tell …," he said. "The ends were so covered in snow and ice. And it could have made them look broken just by dragging them …," his voice trailed off.

Joseph was fully with them now. All sobs and anger were gone. "Then Papa and Thérèse must have been thrown from the sleigh." His voice was pitched high with excitement. "They could be laying there hurt and freezing." He ran to get his coat. "We must ride to the rescue!"

Angelique couldn't help but smile through her worry. Joseph didn't need much excuse to ride to the rescue. She remembered him following her after the horse raiders. That had almost led to disaster. Some rescuer! But she didn't want to discourage him.

"What worries me," she said to François, "is that your parents didn't know they were coming, so your father wouldn't know to go out looking for them if they had an accident." She looked at François.

"*If* they had an accident." François shook his head but he looked worried. "We don't know."

"But," she said softly, "*if* they had an accident ... we are the only ones who know they are out there."

Joseph had wrapped his moccasins around the bottom of his buckskin pants so that they'd be snow-proof. He had his coat and *toque* on and was standing impatiently at the door.

"What are you waiting for?" he demanded. "They could be freezing to death!"

Angelique was only too aware of that. She could see Papa lying pinned beneath the sleigh after Mennwi had dragged it before breaking loose to come home. Poor sick Thérèse was half-buried in snow in the ditch.

"Joseph," she said. She was trying hard to be calm but her voice was breaking. "You haven't been out in the storm. The horses won't want to go into the wind." She couldn't speak—had to stop—she didn't want to break down in front of François and Joseph.

François stood up. "I don't think I'd agree to go except for one thing." He turned to Angelique. "Mennwi and Gurnuy would probably not want to go, but if I can persuade Pisiskees to go, he'll know the way. If I let him have his head, he can find the road even in the storm and he'll want to get home. But …," and he was looking at Joseph now, "you will have to let me tie Gurnuy to my saddle. We have to stay together and let Pisiskees lead."

Angelique nodded. It didn't take any imagination to know that they wouldn't want to lose anyone on a day like this.

"You too," François said to Angelique. "We'll tie Mennwi on too. We can be like a pack train. It's easier for the horses to follow each other."

Again Angelique nodded. She was grateful to François even more for not mentioning the possibility that if Mennwi had shied and tipped the sleigh at a certain place along the road, he might very well shy again. She hadn't ridden him that much and it was one thing to ride a bucking horse on a beautiful fall day. Riding him in the middle of a raging blizzard would be another matter altogether. If he was tied behind Gurnuy, there would be less reason to fear having a problem.

Bracing themselves against the fury of the wind and the snow biting at their faces, they opened the door and headed out to saddle up.

Even an imagination as vivid as Angelique's could not have prepared her for the problems they had setting out. Nobody with any horse sense would go out in this storm. And it seemed that tonight the horses were possessed with more sense than usual.

Saddling and bridling them had not been a problem. Getting them out into the yard and trying to make them move away from the barn certainly was. Again it was François who saved the day. He had his big piebald pony completely under control. Once he persuaded Pisiskees that they were heading home no matter what the weather, the little cavalcade set out.

It was dawn and it was no longer pitch dark. Riding behind Joseph's pony, Angelique could just make out Gurnuy's rump. If anything, the storm was raging even worse than before. Perhaps it just felt that way up here on the horse's back, where she was more exposed to the wind and snow. She pulled up her scarf so that it came almost to her hood. Now there was just a narrow slit to peer through. Even then the snow seemed to find its way in. Her eyelashes were so heavy with frost that she could barely see.

"It's less than a mile," she told herself. She kept repeating it like a prayer. "We can do it … it's less than a mile … less than a mile."

It was hard holding on; the snow was so deep that the horses were plunging into drifts up to their bellies. Sometimes they would slip where the road was icy beneath the snow. She hated to think what would happen if one of the horses fell.

Angelique was tempted to just shut her eyes and hold on, but she kept peering ahead. Sometimes, through the swirling snow, she could make out the dark shape of her brother riding ahead. Good. Joseph was managing to stay on his pony. Thinking about him made her smile. So determined. Most of the time she was annoyed by his stubborn nature, but when it came to something like this, she had to admire him. Once he made up his mind, he would never give up. He wasn't worrying about *Wendigoes* now.

She wondered how far they had come. Up ahead François was riding steadily on. She wished they could call to each other but the screaming of the wind made that impossible.

Then, as if François had read her thoughts, he stopped and turned his horse back toward them. The three animals were close now, Gurnuy still with his head to Pisiskees's rump but François was beside Joseph, his horse's head beside Mennwi's.

"Are you both all right?" François yelled, his voice nearly lost in the wind.

Angelique could see Joseph's head nodding. His mouth was hidden beneath his scarf too. It must be getting lighter if she could see him that well.

"Oui!" she cried as loud as she could, knowing her voice was muffled by the scarf.

François obviously heard her. He reached out and patted Joseph's back in encouragement. *"Bon!"* he yelled turning Pisiskees back into the lead again.

Angelique watched as he was swallowed once more by the storm. She wished she could have asked him if he knew where they were—how far they'd come. But she knew it was useless. He probably wouldn't know anyway, wouldn't have been able to see any landmarks. Even the roadway into his own home probably wouldn't show. They would just have to trust that Pisiskees would know and turn in when they got there.

She patted Mennwi with her mittened hand. "*Bon,* Mennwi," she murmured. He probably wouldn't hear her anyway but it would do no good to scream at him. "*Bon,* Mennwi," she said again.

It was good that it was getting lighter. Now, whenever the snow stopped blowing in her face, she was able to see as far ahead as to where François was. She watched through the narrow slit as his horse lunged into yet another snowdrift.

Mennwi started to dance nervously. What was wrong? He'd followed the others bravely into all the other drifts. Angelique hung on, her mittens slipping on the reins.

"*Bon,* Mennwi," she said again. She couldn't pat him now, she was holding on as he side-stepped skittishly, pulling back on the rope attached to Joseph's horse.

"Whoa!" she yelled. She looked ahead to François for help just as she saw the black shape of the overturned sleigh beside the road ahead.

Now she knew why Mennwi was frightened. He must have been terrified and perhaps even hurt when the sleigh overturned before. She tried to hold him, but he reared back, pulling the rope free. Then he spun about and dashed away. Back, the way they had come.

It was a miracle, Angelique thought, that she had been able to hold on. She knew it was hopeless trying to stop him. Her mittens were too slippery on the icy reins. She was holding on to the saddle with both hands, hoping that she still held the reins as well. Surely Mennwi could not gallop very far at this speed with the snow so deep, even though he was following the track they'd made earlier. He would have to slow down soon. At least he'd do as he'd done before and take her home. If she could stay on his back.

CHAPTER No 11

François watched Angelique and Mennwi disappear into the storm. It had been all he could do to hold his and Joseph's ponies when Mennwi bolted. Luckily, Pisiskees was a good deal bigger than Gurnuy and the rope tied to his saddle had held.

Now François calmed his pony as he rode closer to the overturned sleigh. Pisiskees snorted as he sniffed at it. Joseph had jumped off Gurnuy and run over to the sleigh. He was digging on the other side and François realized there was someone there. He leapt off, tied

Pisiskees's reins to the runner, and went to help.

Louise Dumas was lying partly covered by the sleigh. It was a moment before François realized that he was not alone.

"Joseph!" He knew that he had to calm the boy down. Angelique's brother was frantically trying to get the snow away from his father.

"Joseph, we must get the sleigh off them. We'll tie the ropes onto the sleigh and get our ponies to help pull it off." He was relieved that Joseph seemed to be calm enough to understand. He'd stopped wearing himself out moving snow at least.

"If we lift while they are pulling, we can do it." He wanted to get the boy away, make him feel he was being useful and could make a difference. "Come on!"

Joseph followed and they began to tie the ponies to the runner of the sleigh.

"Can you get the ponies to pull when I give you the signal?" François decided that as the strongest one, he would have a better chance of lifting the sleigh so that it didn't drag across the two people beneath.

Joseph nodded and went to the horses' heads, taking the reins and backing up preparing to pull.

"Geeup!" François waited until he had a glimpse of Joseph pulling and then let out a shrill whistle.

It was a signal Pisiskees knew meant "move now," but it startled Gurnuy too and made him jerk the sleigh so that they began to drag it. It took all of François's strength but he managed to hold up the sleigh, and it flipped over onto its side as it was pulled away.

"Whoa!" yelled François and the horses stood blowing and quivering.

"Papa!" Joseph was beginning to panic again. His father lay very still beneath the buffalo robes that had fallen on him when the sleigh tipped over.

Thérèse was moaning though. François realized that they had probably been protected from being hurt by the thick robes they'd used for

"Papa!" Joseph was beginning to panic again.

cover in the sleigh. Certainly the robes had saved them from freezing in the snow. And the overturned sleigh had protected them from the wind.

"Papa!" Joseph was yelling as he pressed his mittened hands against his father's cheeks. "Papa!" He was crying and calling, nose to nose with the unconscious man.

François decided to leave them and check on Thérèse. She was sitting up looking confused.

"Do you think you could ride the rest of the way?" François asked.

Thérèse nodded and tried to stand. She was not prepared for the wind that greeted her. The sleigh had not been pulled far and served as a windbreak sheltering them from the storm.

"Papa!" Joseph had not given up and now his persistence was rewarded.

Louie Dumas opened his eyes and smiled at his son. "Did I ever tell you that you are a very noisy boy?"

Joseph was laughing and crying now. "Oh, Papa!" he said throwing himself on his father.

"I hope you are not injured," François asked. He wasn't sure if he should be pulling Joseph away or if he should just let Joseph have his moment.

Monsieur Dumas shook his head and then put his hand to it, grimacing in pain. "I must have banged my head, but otherwise I think I have no broken bones." He looked over to where Thérèse leaned against the tipped sleigh. "Oh, Thérèse, what a terrible thing to happen to you."

Thérèse was holding her stomach, but she managed to force a slight smile. "I will be all right." She said, "François is going to let me ride his horse the rest of the way …"

"And you can ride Gurnuy, Papa!" Joseph could hardly contain himself. "And I will lead you … and Pisiskees knows the way even in the storm … and we must be nearly there … don't you think so, François?" With that Joseph seemed to run out of breath. He looked expectantly at François.

François had already gone to untie the ponies from the sleigh and was bringing them around.

"I think it might be better if your papa rode my Pisiskees and Thérèse rode your pony. She is not so heavy."

Joseph looked disappointed but he didn't argue.

François could see Thérèse look longingly back at the heavy buffalo robes when the full fury of the wind hit her, but she climbed onto Gurnuy without a word, bending her head into the wind as they set out.

It was not until they were on their way that Louise Dumas asked about his daughter. "Where is Angelique?" he said. "I'm surprised that she didn't insist on coming along!"

CHAPTER No 12

Mennwi was still going full gallop when he hit an icy spot on the road. As he stumbled and slid, Angelique had no doubt that he would lose his footing and pitch forward. Better to let go and jump rather than risk being crushed beneath him.

"Now!" Angelique said to herself as the horse seemed ready to fall. She loosened her grip on the saddle and threw herself off into the snowbank.

She landed headfirst, but the snow was so deep, it was like landing face down in a big pillow.

A cold, wet pillow. Her eyes were full of snow and she couldn't see a thing. She pawed at her face with her mittens until she cleared most of the snow away. But now her face was wet and freezing beneath her scarf.

She started to scramble out of the snow. She must try to see where Mennwi had fallen and get to him before he got up. If only he hadn't broken a leg. Like Michif. Her eyes filled with tears, remembering the horse she loved.

"Oh, Michif," she wanted to throw herself down and weep but she didn't dare. She had to get to Mennwi so she could get back on. She kept rubbing her eyes so that she could see again. But no matter where she looked there was no sign of Mennwi. The horse was gone. Run away.

She was alone in the storm and she didn't know where she was. All she could see was snow. The wind bit at her eyes. Tears would be frozen onto her face.

It seemed as if the wind couldn't decide which way it was coming from now. Snow blew at her from above and beneath and sideways. There was no way to turn her head from it, no way to know by the direction of the wind which way she should go to find her way home. It would be best to go home, Angelique decided.

François and Joseph would have found Papa and Thérèse if they were still with the sleigh. Unless they were terribly hurt, they would get them to the LaVallées' house. They had two horses. They would be all right. No point in turning back. She had no idea how far Mennwi had carried her. Home might be just around the corner. She would try to follow Mennwi's tracks since she would never be able to find the road home otherwise. She could not see anything in the tempest of snow.

She could barely see her feet but in the dim light she could see the horse's tracks. The trail that their horses had made earlier was almost obliterated by the drifting snow. Mennwi's tracks would be gone soon too. She bent low so that she could see Mennwi's tracks and because it protected her a little from the fury of the wind. The snow lashed at her eyes. She would have pulled up her scarf again but was afraid to touch it. What if it came loose? Her hands were too cold to tie it again. The wind might just whip it out of her hands and her face would be unprotected.

She stumbled along. Where the drifts were deep, she sometimes felt as if all she was doing was lifting her feet and bringing them down in the same place.

And she was tired. She was so very, very tired.

If only Michif were here. He would not have left her to walk. She reminded herself that Michif was gone. Dead. There was no Michif to help her. At least she was too tired to cry.

Her legs felt heavy. It was as if she were wearing stones instead of moccasins. Moccasins didn't weigh this much. You could run and run in moccasins and never get tired. She looked down, expecting to see rocks on her feet. But she was sure they were moccasins. Why were they so heavy? Maybe they were rocks painted to look like moccasins. She could hardly lift them. She fell face forward in the snow.

She was cold, but lying here at least the wind wasn't biting at her so much. She snuggled down. The snow was like a soft bed. She rolled over and lay there looking up. Above her the snow was blowing across but she was safe down here. She could see it beginning to drift right over her. It would fill in and cover her like a blanket and she would be warm at last.

She closed her eyes.

CHAPTER No 13

"Angelique came with us—" François began.

Joseph interrupted. "She was riding Mennwi and he shied at the sleigh and he ran away with her … but Angelique didn't fall off … she's a very good rider … and Mennwi would just run home again," Joseph actually paused for breath. "He ran home before," he said. "That's how we knew to come looking for you … at least François and Angelique knew something had happened. I was the one who said we should come," he finished proudly.

"That's right," François said when he had a chance. "I'm sure she'll be fine. She's smart. She'll know enough to stay home once she gets there."

Joseph's papa nodded. "She's smart, our Angelique," he said. "You are right there." But he sounded worried.

François had been right. Though the storm raged on and the snow swirled about them so they couldn't see, Pisiskees suddenly veered to the left and started to move more quickly.

"We're almost home!" François said. "Well done, Pisiskees!" he patted the big pony as it broke into a trot. There was a barn somewhere ahead and as far as he was concerned he would go no farther.

Sure enough, they could soon smell the smoke from the house and then the glow of light from the windows shone dimly through the storm.

The boys left Thérèse and Monsieur Dumas at the door to the LaVallées' home and led their faithful steeds to the warmth and shelter of the barn.

Sometime later François came in, brushing off the snow.

"But where is Joseph?" his maman asked looking worried. "We have one of our heroes here but where is the other?"

François laughed. "He's still rubbing down that pony of his … you would think Gurnuy was the greatest horse in the world!"

But Joseph did not come in. And eventually his worried papa went to the barn to look for him.

There was no sign of either boy or pony.

CHAPTER No. 14

Angelique felt lovely and warm now. She knew she should get up and continue walking home. But she would just lie here a little longer. She needed to rest anyway. She would walk the rest of the way when her feet didn't feel so heavy.

She felt so peaceful here. Floating. As if she were an angel sitting on a fluffy cloud. The storm would be over soon. Then she would go.

Maybe in the spring the snow would melt, and she would get up and go home then.

Spring was nice. But the angels she'd made, the lovely angels, would be gone. She had wanted to show them to Maman. She'd better get up as soon as she rested a bit more.

"Go away!" she said.

Something was touching her, moving her nice snow blanket away.

"Go away!" louder this time.

She opened her eyes. A white face above her. Aaah. Of course. It was an angel come to share her cloud. *All right,* she thought, moving a little. She would share it but the angel had better stop poking her.

She looked again. She'd thought angels' faces were smooth like those in the pictures. But then she'd never seen a real angel before. This one's face was covered like the trees when the branches bristled with hoar frost. Very pretty.

"Angelique!" the angel said.

Of course an angel would know her name. She just didn't understand how it could speak when there was no mouth. The face was just like a frosty mask. Except for the eyes. Brown eyes peered through the white frost. Did angels have brown eyes? In the holy pictures Thérèse had, they were blue. What kind of an angel was this? And why did it keep poking and pulling at her?

"Angelique! Get up!"

The angel's voice was too loud now. Most un-angelic. She wasn't going to let such a noisy, pushy angel share her cloud.

"Go away!" she said.

Angelique decided she would have to get up and get rid of this angel once and for all. She tried to sit up but she felt too stiff. The angel was still pulling insistently. Somehow she sat up.

The wind was so strong, she almost fell back. Suddenly she was cold, so very, very cold. She was not on a cloud at all.

"Angelique, come on! Get up!"

She was being pushed. Somehow she was standing on her stone feet and there was a pony. Joseph's pony.

"Climb on, Angelique!" Joseph's voice, crying. Begging her. "I can't lift you, Angelique! You have to do it!" Pleading now.

Luckily, Gurnuy was a small pony. She could never have climbed on but somehow, with her leaning across the pony's back and Joseph pushing, she was on. Lying on her stomach, arms dangling on one side, legs on the other.

"Gurnuy knows the way home," Joseph said proudly.

It seemed everyone was there. The little Dumas cabin was filled with people when Angelique opened her eyes.

Vaguely she remembered Joseph pulling her off the pony and pushing her into the house. The stove had not gone out and it seemed blessedly warm and safe to her. Joseph had managed to get the fire blazing again.

Not long after that Papa and Madame LaVallée had arrived. Angelique had been bundled up in a warm, dry bed. She vaguely remembered her feet being bathed and Madame pronouncing that the frostbite was not too severe. And then Angelique had slept.

She had slept through all these people coming. The storm was over. Maman and *Pchit* Rose were here. And Thérèse looking pale but smiling as she sat with her cup of tea. One for Angelique too. Very sweet to give her strength, Madame LaVallée said.

Seeing Angelique was awake, Maman brought the *bebé* over to lie beside her sister.

Joseph was there too, resting and being fussed over.

But she had to ask him. "How did you find me?"

"You were almost buried and I would have missed you," he said, "but Gurnuy started snorting and pulling away so I knew there was something there … I was just going to come home and make sure Mennwi had brought you there … but then I thought I'd look, and I could see something was buried in the snowdrift so I poked and you said, 'Go away!' in a cranky voice, so I knew it was you." He looked at her reproachfully. "You were awfully hard to get moving, Angelique."

Angelique smiled at her brother. He was definitely no angel, but he'd have to do.

Glossary of Michif Words

page 2: *kokum*
Translation: grandmother
Note: This is a Cree word.

page 2: *Wendigo*
Note: This name does not have a direct translation. It is derived from the Algonkian root word *witiku* and means "evil spirit" and "cannibal." The Algonkian people include the Mi'kmaq, Montagnais-Naskapi, Algonkin, Ojibwa, Cree, and Blackfoot. Thus, the *Wendigo* haunts the forests and tundra from the Atlantic Ocean in the east, across to the Rocky Mountains in the west, and north to the Arctic Ocean. The *Wendigo* is known to take the form of a half-phantom, half-beast that roams the forest, feasts on flesh and blood, scares people to death with a single look, is made of stone or of ice, and has supernatural strength and speed. The *Wendigo* can be thought of as an explanation for the unknown. It can also be seen as a nursery bogey to teach children to "behave or the *Wendigo* will get you!"

page 4: Gurnuy
Translation: frog
Note: This is Michif for "frog," from the French *grenouille*.

page 4: La Griz
Translation: the Grey One
Note: This is in Michif.

page 5: Mennwi
Translation: midnight
Note: This is Michif for "midnight," from the French *minuit*.

page 6: *kinik-kinik*
Translation: bear berry
Note: This plant is sometimes used as tobacco.

page 9: *bonswer*
Translation: good evening
Note: This is the Michif equivalent for the French *bonsoir*.

page 10: *"Kikwaay ispayin?"*
Translation: "What's happening?"
Note: This is in Michif.

page 14: *lii chiran*
Translation: the Northern Lights
Note: This is Michif for "the Northern Lights," from the French *les tirants*.

page 16: *siru d'pwer*
Translation: saskatoon berry syrup
Note: This is Michif for "saskatoon berry syrup."

page 18: *"Enn pchit fiiy!"*
Translation: "A baby girl!"
Note: This is Michif for "a baby girl," from the French *une petite fille*.

page 21: *bonnom di niizh*
Translation: snowman
Note: This is Michif for "snowman," from the French *bonhomme de neige*.

page 22: *jaeng*
Translation: boyfriend
Note: This is Michif for "boyfriend," "girlfriend," "fiancé," or "fiancée."

page 28: *enn patak*

Translation: a potato

Note: This is Michif for "a potato," from the French *une pataque.*

page 30: *en zweezuu d'niizh*

Translation: a snowbird

Note: This is Michif for "snowbird," from the French *un oiseau de neige.*

page 35: *glissantes*

Translation: dumplings

Note: This is Michif for "dumplings," from the French *glissante,* meaning "slippery."

page 40: *"Collinn!"*

Translation: "Darn!"

Note: This Michif word doesn't have a direct translation. "Darn!" is close though.

page 50: *maarsi*

Translation: thank you

Note: This is Michif for "thank you," from the French *merci.*

Bibliography

Anderson, Frank. *The Riel Rebellion—1885* (Surrey, B.C.: Frontier Books, 1985).

Barkwell, Lawrence J., Leah Dorion, and Darren R. Prefontaine. *Resources for Metis Researchers* (Winnipeg: Gabriel Dumont Institute and Manitoba Metis Federation, 1999).

Barnholden, Michael (trans.). *Gabriel Dumont Speaks* (Vancouver: Talonbooks, 1993).

Lussier, Antoine S., and D. Bruce Sealey. *The Other Natives: The Metis, Vol. III* (Winnipeg: Manitoba Metis Federation Press and Editions Bois Brules, 1980).

Lusty, Terrance W.J. *Metis Social-Political Movement* (Calgary: N.W. Printing, 1973).

Payment, Diane. *Batoche (1870–1910)* (Saint Boniface, Man.: Les Editions du Ble, 1983).

Payment, Diane. *Les Gens Libres—Otipemisiwak: Batoche, Saskatchewan, 1870–1930: Etudes en archeologie et histoire* (Ottawa: Service des parcs Canada, 1990).

Silver, Alfred. *Lord of the Plains* (New York: Ballantyne Books, 1990).

Van Kirk, Sylvia. *Many Tender Ties* (Winnipeg: Watson & Dwyer, 1993).

Woodcock, George. *Gabriel Dumont: The Metis Chief and His Lost World* (Edmonton: Hurtig Publishers, 1975).

Acknowledgements

Special thanks to Professor Robert A. Papen for his help with the Michif translations.

Thank you to Rise Fleury of Duck Lake for coming up with a suitable cuss word in Michif for Angelique to use!

Thanks to Jocelyn Mant for reading the manuscript for me.

I am, as always, grateful to my husband, Earl Georgas, for his love and support (and proof-reading!).

Dear Reader,

This has been the fourth and final book about Angelique. We hope you've enjoyed meeting and getting to know her as much as we have enjoyed bringing her—and her wonderful story—to you.

Although Angelique's tale is told, there are still eleven more terrific girls to read about, whose exciting adventures take place in Canada's past—girls just like you. So do keep on reading!

And please—don't forget to keep in touch! We love receiving your incredible letters telling us about your favourite stories and which girls you like best. And thank you for telling us about the stories you would like to read! There are so many remarkable stories in Canadian history. It seems that wherever we live, great stories live too, in our towns and cities, on our rivers and mountains. We hope that Our Canadian Girl *captures the richness of that past.*

Sincerely,
Barbara Berson
Editor

Canada's

1608
Samuel de Champlain establishes the first fortified trading post at Quebec.

1755
The British expel the entire French population of Acadia (today's Maritime provinces), sending them into exile.

1759
The British defeat the French in the Battle of the Plains of Abraham.

1776
The 13 Colonies revolt against Britain, and the Loyalists flee to Canada.

1812
The United States declares war against Canada.

1837
Calling for responsible government, the Patriotes, following Louis-Joseph Papineau, rebel in Lower Canada; William Lyon Mackenzie leads the uprising in Upper Canada.

1845
The expedition of Sir John Franklin to the Arctic ends when the ship is frozen in the pack ice; the fate of its crew remains a mystery.

1867
New Brunswick, Nova Scotia, and the United Province of Canada come together in Confederation to form the Dominion of Canada.

1869
Louis Riel leads his Metis followers in the Red River Rebellion.

1870
Manitoba joins Canada. The Northwest Territories become an official territory of Canada.

1871
British Columbia joins Canada.

1870
Angelique

Timeline

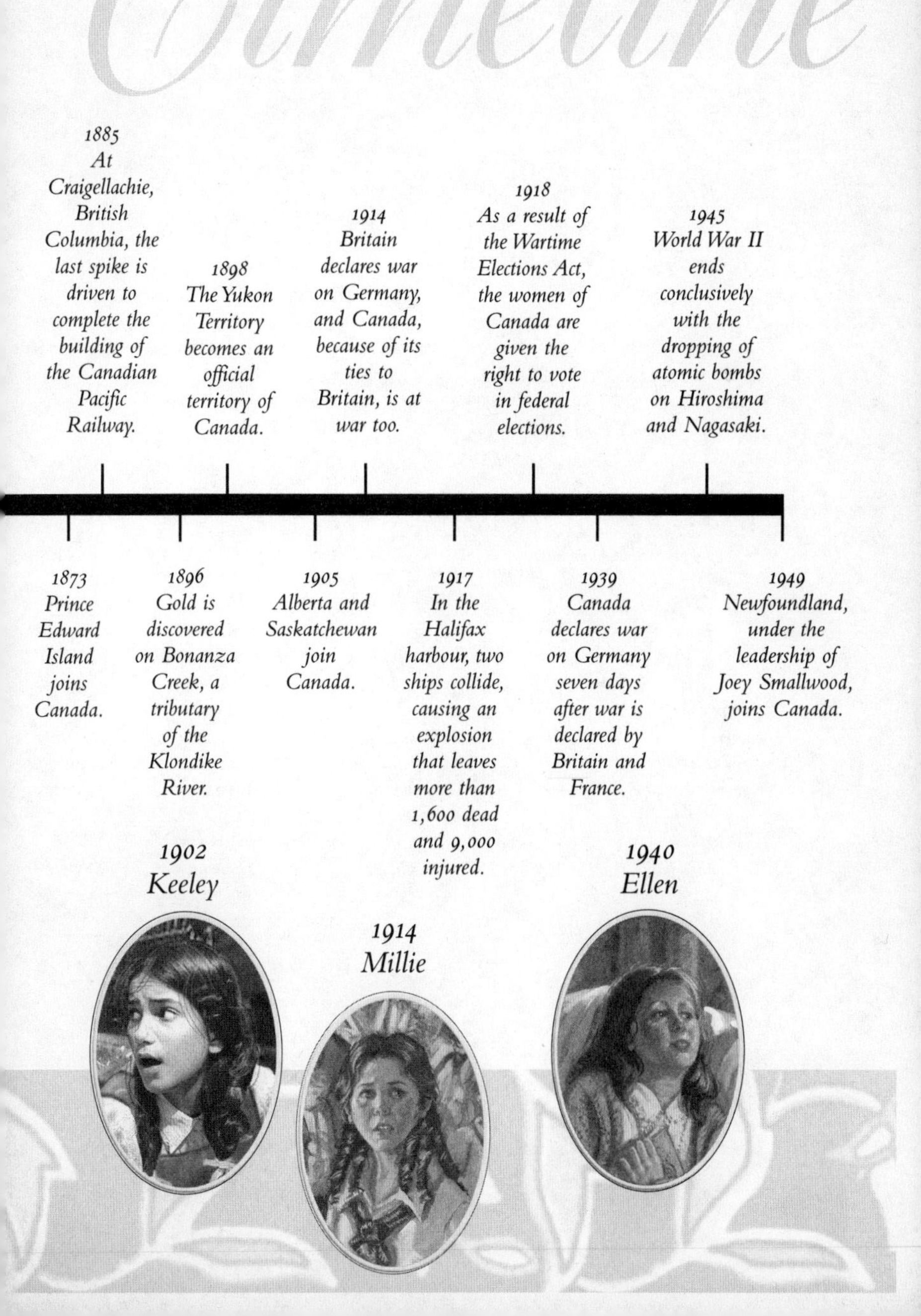
1873
Prince Edward Island joins Canada.
1885
At Craigellachie, British Columbia, the last spike is driven to complete the building of the Canadian Pacific Railway.
1896
Gold is discovered on Bonanza Creek, a tributary of the Klondike River.
1898
The Yukon Territory becomes an official territory of Canada.
1902
Keeley
1905
Alberta and Saskatchewan join Canada.
1914
Britain declares war on Germany, and Canada, because of its ties to Britain, is at war too.
1914
Millie
1917
In the Halifax harbour, two ships collide, causing an explosion that leaves more than 1,600 dead and 9,000 injured.
1918
As a result of the Wartime Elections Act, the women of Canada are given the right to vote in federal elections.
1939
Canada declares war on Germany seven days after war is declared by Britain and France.
1940
Ellen
1945
World War II ends conclusively with the dropping of atomic bombs on Hiroshima and Nagasaki.
1949
Newfoundland, under the leadership of Joey Smallwood, joins Canada.